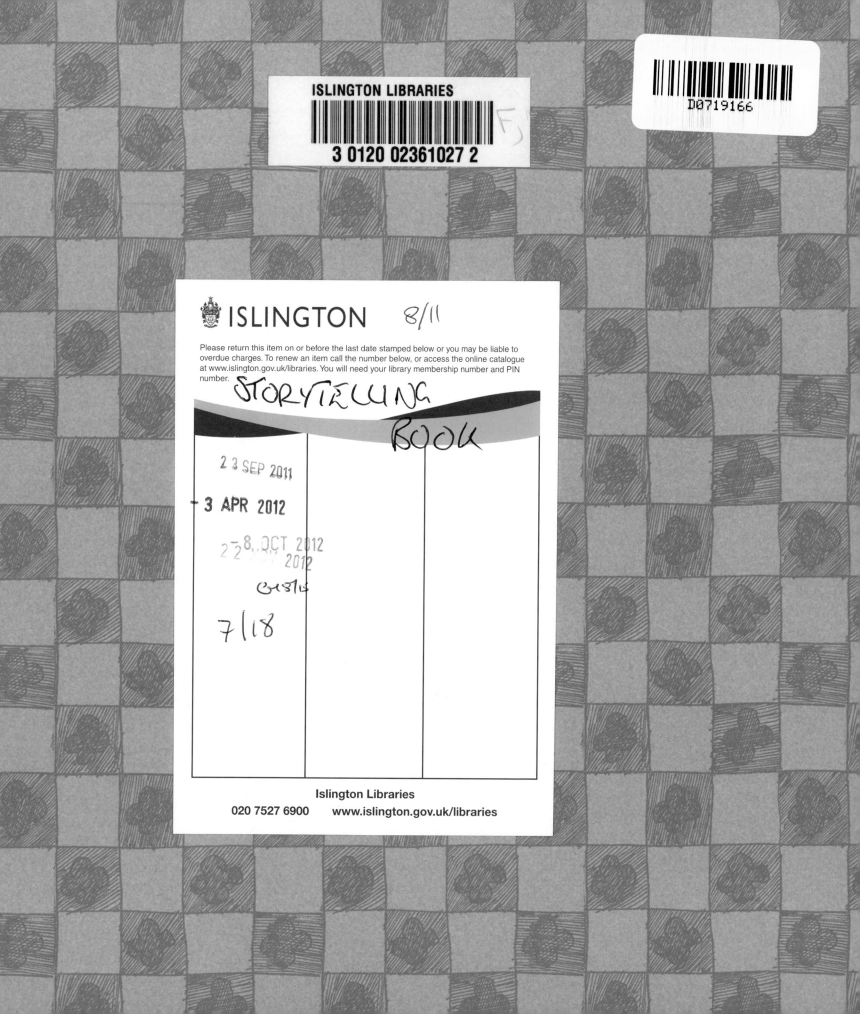

The King of
Quizzical Island
Digs Through
the World

*For dearest Maeve,
who makes our own world such a delight.
With all my love and thanks ~ G. S.*

For Satoshi Motoko ~ D. McK.

First published 2011 by Walker Books Ltd
87 Vauxhall Walk, London SE11 5HJ

2 4 6 8 10 9 7 5 3 1

Text © 2011 Gordon Snell
Illustrations © 2011 David McKee

This book has been typeset in Avenir Light

Printed in China

British Library Cataloguing in Publication Data:
a catalogue record for this book is available from the British Library

ISBN 978-1-4063-1214-0

www.walker.co.uk

The King of Quizzical Island
Digs Through the World

Gordon Snell   illustrated by David McKee

WALKER BOOKS
AND SUBSIDIARIES
LONDON • BOSTON • SYDNEY • AUCKLAND

The King of Quizzical Island

Can never be left in doubt.

If a question is asked in his kingdom,

He must find the answer out...

And so when the old Owl asked him,

"Can you prove that the world is round?"

He made a spade with a diamond blade

And began to dig in the ground.

He said, "You'll know that the world is round

And the fact can't be denied,

When I've dug a tunnel right through it

And come out at the other side!"

The Whispering Witches whimpered;

The Owl got quite hysterical.

He said, "Supposing you dig through the world

And find it isn't spherical?"

But the King just went on digging,

While his puzzled gardeners frowned;

They said, "If he's planting cabbages,

They're much too deep in the ground."

"It's never been done!" cried the Wizard,

"Not once in a new blue moon."

But from deep, deep down in the hole in the ground,

A voice called, "See you soon!"

_____

The King dug on with his singular spade,

Till his feet got a shaky feeling –

Then all at once he tumbled down

Through a hole in somebody's ceiling.

The King looked all around him,

But he seemed to be quite alone

In a wide and vaulted chamber

With pillars of polished bone.

Then suddenly, from the rafters,

A clatter of bones fell down –

And the King saw, sprawled before him,

A Skeleton, wearing a crown.

"You are welcome, sir," said the figure

In deep and doleful tones –

"I am the Monarch of Calcium,

And this is my Kingdom of Bones.

"I have bones from mammoths and mastodons,

Werewolves and warlocks too;

Mice and mermaids and marmosets –

But none from a King like you."

He picked up a silver sickle

And flung it towards the King.

The curved blade whirled like a boomerang

And flashed like a swallow's wing.

The King ducked out of the sickle's path,

And onward the bright blade sped –

With a boomerang turn it sailed right back

And cut off the Skeleton's head!

The King dug deeper and deeper

Till his tunnel came right through

To a tall and chilly cavern,

Where a Giant blocked the view.

His head was pressed to the ceiling

On a cork that was huge and round.

He said, "I must keep this cork in place,

Or the Underworld will be drowned.

"For above us here is ocean –

The cork is the only plug.

If I let go and the ocean drains,

Imagine the GLUG-GLUG-GLUG!

"The waters will gush and tumble,

Gurgle and splash and spread,

While ships get stuck and fishes gasp

On the dried-up ocean bed."

The King said, "You do noble work!"

And the Giant replied, with a sob,

"That may be so, but to tell the truth,

It's a terribly boring job!"

So the King built a pile of boulders

As high as the Giant's head.

He said, "Now take a bit of a break –

Let these stones do the job instead."

He wedged the final stone in place

And it held the cork plug fast.

Said the Giant, "I've stood for a million years –

It's good to sit down at last!"

The Giant dozed off, and the King dug on

Till he came to a curious lair

Where a Dinosaur and a Dragon

Each sat in a large armchair.

The King remarked to the Dinosaur,

"I thought you were extinct!"

"Do I look it?" the big beast grumbled;

"What a stupid thought to have think'd!

"I moved here when the Ice Age came

And I felt the hailstones strike me."

Said the Dragon, "I came to escape Saint George –

He didn't seem to like me!"

"The trouble is that the ceiling's low,"

The Dinosaur sadly said,

"And it causes an earthquake up above

Whenever I bump my head."

Said the Dragon, "Your scientists are clever,

But there's something not even *they* know:

I breathe fire through the holes in this ceiling

To make what you call a volcano!"

The King said farewell, and dug onwards

Through rocks too old to name;

He plunged through oceans of boiling mud

And swam sizzling seas of flame.

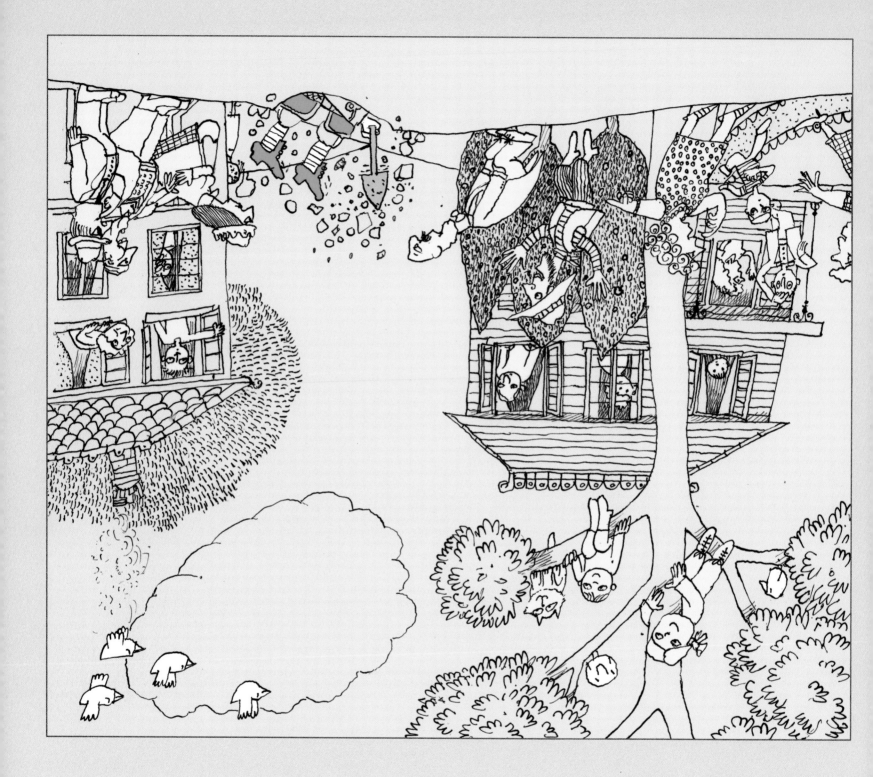

At last, he came out in the open air

And gazed, from beneath his crown,

At a land where the earth was above the sky

And the people walked upside-down.

"Then it's true!" he cried, as he heard the cheers

Of the topsy-turvy folk;

"I must hurry home to my subjects,

And tell them it's not a joke.

"The world *is* round, and I've proved it!"

  But the people said, with a frown,

"It is, but *we* are the right way up –

  It's *you* who are upside-down!"

"I suppose," said the King politely,

"It depends which side you are on!

  Well, I've really enjoyed our meeting,

  But now it's time I was gone."

He waved goodbye and went back again
The way that he'd come before,
Through rocks and mud and sizzling seas
To the Dragon and Dinosaur.

"Can't stop!" he called, as they greeted him,
"For now I am homeward bound –
I'll go back to Quizzical Island
And tell them the world is round."

He went past the sleeping Giant

And the headless Skeleton too,

And emerged, exclaiming, "Hello! It's me!"

And his people cried, "It's you!"

Everyone cheered and shouted;

They sang and they played the fiddle:

Their King had proved that the world is round

By digging right through the middle.

But the Owl thought, "What if the earth's a cube

One thousand and one miles wide?

You could still dig right through the middle

And come out at the other side."

The King knew the Owl was doubtful,

But he said, "Let's celebrate!

Your geometrical quibbles

Will simply have to wait!"

There were banquets and processions,

Ten thousand flags unfurled,

And bonfires burned for the King who'd returned

From the other side of the world.

The people, they gasped in wonder.

They said, "Gosh!" and "Gulp!" and "Glory!"

At the King who'd gone digging into the world

And come back to tell the story.